The Boxcar Children Mysteries

THE BOXCAR CHILDREN
SURPRISE ISLAND
THE YELLOW HOUSE MYSTERY
MYSTERY RANCH
MIKE'S MYSTERY
BLUE BAY MYSTERY
THE WOODSHED MYSTERY
THE LIGHTHOUSE MYSTERY
MOUNTAIN TOP MYSTERY
SCHOOLHOUSE MYSTERY
CABOOSE MYSTERY
HOUSEBOAT MYSTERY
SNOWBOUND MYSTERY
TREE HOUSE MYSTERY
BICYCLE MYSTERY
MYSTERY IN THE SAND
MYSTERY BEHIND THE WALL
BUS STATION MYSTERY
BENNY UNCOVERS A MYSTERY
THE HAUNTED CABIN
  MYSTERY
THE DESERTED LIBRARY
  MYSTERY
THE ANIMAL SHELTER
  MYSTERY
THE OLD MOTEL MYSTERY
THE MYSTERY OF THE HIDDEN
  PAINTING
THE AMUSEMENT PARK
  MYSTERY
THE MYSTERY OF THE MIXED-
  UP ZOO

THE CAMP-OUT MYSTERY
THE MYSTERY GIRL
THE MYSTERY CRUISE
THE DISAPPEARING FRIEND
  MYSTERY
THE MYSTERY OF THE SINGING
  GHOST
MYSTERY IN THE SNOW
THE PIZZA MYSTERY
THE MYSTERY HORSE
THE MYSTERY AT THE DOG
  SHOW
THE CASTLE MYSTERY
THE MYSTERY OF THE LOST
  VILLAGE
THE MYSTERY ON THE ICE
THE MYSTERY OF THE
  PURPLE POOL
THE GHOST SHIP MYSTERY
THE MYSTERY IN
  WASHINGTON, DC
THE CANOE TRIP MYSTERY
THE MYSTERY OF THE HIDDEN
  BEACH
THE MYSTERY OF THE MISSING
  CAT
THE MYSTERY AT SNOWFLAKE
  INN
THE MYSTERY ON STAGE
THE DINOSAUR MYSTERY
THE MYSTERY OF THE STOLEN
  MUSIC

THE PANTHER MYSTERY

created by
GERTRUDE CHANDLER WARNER

Illustrated by Charles Tang

ALBERT WHITMAN & Company
Morton Grove, Illinois

ISBN 0-8075-6328-5

1 3 5 7 9 10 8 6 4 2

Printed in the U.S.A.

Contents

CHAPTER 1

The Pink Hotel

Violet Alden saw the little hotel first. "Oh, it's so pretty! Like a sunset!" She was sitting in the front seat with Grandfather.

"You're right, Violet. The Flamingo Hotel certainly lives up to its name! I've never seen such a bright pink!" Grandfather steered the rental car into the driveway.

Six-year-old Benny Alden leaned out a window. "I'm going to climb that tree and get a coconut!" he exclaimed. "It's a pretty short tree."

"That's because it's a palmetto, not a palm tree," said Henry, reading from a guidebook.

After the Alden family had landed at the Miami airport, Benny had rushed to the windows to watch planes take off, but Henry had headed for a little bookstand. At fourteen, he was becoming interested in science.

"I bet there are a zillion bugs around here. I'm glad I brought insect spray," remarked twelve-year-old Jessie.

"*This* time I didn't forget my camera!" Violet said. "Florida is a perfect place to take lots of pictures." Violet was ten. When she wasn't drawing, she was snapping photos with her camera.

Grandfather pulled into a parking space near the pink-painted railing of the small porch. "Well, here we are," he said.

"When do we eat?" Benny asked.

Everyone laughed. "We just got here!"

"What happened to the burger and fries you had at the airport?" asked Grandfather.

"That was a long time ago," Benny said.

"Yeah!" said Henry. "Like about thirty minutes ago." With Jessie's help, he began dragging luggage from the trunk.

"It seems hard to believe we're still in the United States," Jessie commented. "I mean, we left Connecticut this morning and now we're in Miami and it doesn't look *anything* like home!"

"I know what you mean," Violet agreed. "Our lawn in Greenfield was smooth and green and Mrs. McGregor's roses were just blooming. But here it's like a *jungle*."

"Wait'll we see the Everglades," Henry added.

"I want to see lots of alligators," put in Benny. "I wished on a star last night."

"I hope we see Andrew Beldon," said Grandfather. "That's the purpose of this trip, after all."

Just yesterday James Alden had received a phone call from a business friend. Thomas Beldon was concerned about his youngest son, Andrew.

Andrew Beldon was a wildlife ranger in the Everglades National Park in south

Florida. Andrew always called his father once a week. But sometimes he got too involved in something and forgot to call. It had been over two weeks since Mr. Beldon had heard from Andrew, and he was too ill to take a trip to Florida. Grandfather had decided that this was a perfect time to visit the Everglades. He could take a vacation with his grandchildren and check on Andrew. He had known Andrew Beldon since Andrew was a boy Benny's age. It wasn't like Andrew to cause his ill father needless worry.

So the Aldens packed and flew to Florida.

"It seems like we're always on the go," Jessie remarked as they carried their luggage up the cement porch steps.

"Maybe it's because we once lived in a boxcar," Henry said thoughtfully. "Even though the boxcar didn't go anywhere, *we've* gone lots of places since Grandfather found us."

After the children's parents died, they had no home. Afraid of the grandfather they had never met, the children lived in an old boxcar in the woods. When James Alden found his grandchildren, he was overjoyed to have a brand-new family.

"But the boxcar *did* go someplace," Benny pointed out.

"That's right," said Violet. "Grandfather had our old boxcar brought to his backyard so we can play in it."

The screen door opened and a small dark-haired woman held it open for them, smiling. "You must be the Aldens. I'm Mrs. Ethel Johnson. Welcome to the Sunshine State!"

They all filed into the cool hallway and set the luggage down.

Grandfather went over to the small registration desk to sign in and chat with Mrs. Johnson.

After being in the bright sun, the children blinked at the dim interior.

From the darkness came a sudden loud cry. *"Hello!"*

Violet was so startled, she nearly dropped her tote bag. "What . . . ?"

Ethel Johnson waved a hand. "Oh, pay no

attention to Mollie. She just wants to be noticed."

As their eyes adjusted to the dim light, the kids realized the screamer was a red parrot on a tall perch.

"Wow!" Benny cried. "What a big beak she has! I bet she eats a lot!"

"Only nuts and seeds," said Ethel. "And animal crackers."

"Does she say different things?" Jessie asked. She thought the bird was beautiful.

"When she's in the mood," Mrs. Johnson replied. "Now I'll take you to your rooms. This is a little hotel. I hope you don't mind sharing two baths."

"Not at all," said Grandfather. "Your place is charming."

"How nice of you to say so," Mrs. Johnson said, leading them down a long hall. "There are five rooms. I've put you in three, all in the back, so you can see the sunrise. The girls are in here and the boys are next door. Mr. Alden is across the hall. Right now, you are my only guests."

"Thank you," Grandfather said.

"If you need anything, just give a yell," shouted Mrs. Johnson on her way back down the hall.

As soon as the woman was down the stairs, Jessie began giggling.

"What's so funny?" Henry asked.

"No wonder the parrot is so loud," Jessie said between giggles. "He learned to yell from Mrs. Johnson."

They all went into their rooms to unpack. The rooms were cheerfully decorated with prints of the Florida Everglades.

"It looks like a swamp," said Benny, staring at the picture over his bed.

"It isn't, really," Henry told him. "It's more like a river, with this long grass growing in it. You'll see. We'll go there tomorrow."

"I wish we could go today," Benny said. "I want to see an alligator."

Just then Grandfather passed their door. "There you all are. I want to make some calls to Andrew and the visitors' center where he works before the Everglades Park closes."

"What about dinner?" Benny said, alligators suddenly forgotten.

"We'll eat in a while, after I make the calls," Grandfather told him. "Why don't you kids go for a walk? It's been a long trip, first on the plane, then driving out from the city. You could use the exercise."

"Great idea," said Violet. "Let's take a look at our neighborhood."

The sun was just beginning to slide over the stately royal palms that lined the street. The air smelled sweet from flowers.

"I'd love to live here," said Jessie, picking a trumpet-shaped blossom and tucking it behind one ear. "It would be like summer all the time."

"But wouldn't you miss the leaves falling?" said Violet.

"And snow?" Henry put in.

"And Watch? And Mrs. McGregor?" Benny added.

Jessie laughed. "All right! All right! I'm not moving to Florida!"

They strolled down the block. The houses were similar in style to the Flamingo

Hotel. A few had signs out front advertising rooms for rent. At the end of the street was another small hotel called simply Seashells.

A man sat on the porch swing, reading a newspaper.

Violet noticed he had bushy brownish hair. He needed a haircut.

As if he read her mind, the man slowly lowered the newspaper. He stared at the Aldens.

"Hello," Violet said shyly.

"Nice evening, isn't it?" Henry added pleasantly.

"Hrmmpf," was all the man said, and went back to his newspaper.

"I wonder what's wrong with him?" Jessie whispered as they turned around and went back to their own hotel.

"Maybe he hasn't had his dinner yet," Benny said.

"I got the hint, Benny," said Henry. "Race you back!"

The kids were red-faced and sweaty when they reached the pink-painted porch.

Grandfather was waiting for them.

"Are we going to dinner now?" Benny asked hopefully. "I wish I could have fried shrimp."

"Yes, Benny," Grandfather said. "We're going to dinner and you may have fried shrimp."

Grandfather looked tired, Jessie thought. And worried. "What is it?" she asked.

"I called the visitors' center where Andrew Beldon works," James Alden said. "They haven't heard from him, either. And there was no answer at Andrew's house."

"You mean he hasn't gone to work?" Henry asked.

Grandfather shook his head. "He hasn't called in sick or taken a leave of absence."

Jessie drew in a breath. "It's like he's disappeared!"

What had happened to Ranger Beldon?

CHAPTER 2

The River of Grass

Mrs. Johnson told the Aldens about a pancake restaurant just down the road. Over pecan pancakes and fresh Florida orange juice the next morning, the Aldens made plans.

"Now what do we do?" asked Violet.

"We're going to the Everglades," James Alden replied. "To the visitors' center where Andrew was supposed to be working. The young woman I spoke to yesterday didn't sound too concerned."

"How did she sound?" Violet asked.

"Annoyed," Grandfather said. "Are we ready to go?" he asked.

"Yes!" the children answered at once.

It was very hot, even early in the morning. The kids were glad their rental car had air-conditioning. Jessie sat up front with Grandfather as his "map guide."

"We just go out Route Forty-one," she told him. "And we come to the Shark Valley Information Center."

"What a funny name," Violet remarked. "They don't have sharks in the Everglades, do they?"

"Not *in* the Everglades," Henry replied. "But there are plenty of sharks in the water around Florida."

Soon they turned into Shark Valley. They parked and went inside the information center. At the front desk, they were greeted by a ranger. Her name badge read, MELANIE HARPER.

"Can I help you?" the young woman asked. She had blond hair cut very short.

"Yes," said Grandfather. "I'm looking

for Andrew Beldon. I understand he works here."

Melanie frowned. "Were you the gentleman who called yesterday?"

"Yes," replied Grandfather. "Andrew is a family friend. I've come to see him."

"Good luck," Melanie said breezily. "He's on rotation here this week, but we haven't seen him. So I'm doing his job as well as mine."

"Andrew hasn't called his supervisor?" asked Grandfather.

"Nope."

Melanie seemed awfully casual, Jessie thought. "Isn't anybody worried about him?" she asked Melanie.

"It's his life," the young woman replied flippantly. "If he wants to lose his job, that's his business."

Henry thought the ranger had the wrong attitude. "Maybe he's sick at home. Has anyone called or gone to his house to check on him?"

"Look, all I know is I have to run Andrew's tram tours and announce the showings of the film," said Melanie. "It isn't easy doing double duty. Now, if you'll excuse me, I have to get ready for the next tour."

The Aldens moved away from the desk and went over to the exhibit area.

"Now I'm really worried," said Grandfather. "But I don't want to call Thomas and tell him that no one has seen Andrew in days. It might make his illness worse."

"You won't have to do that," said Henry firmly. "We'll find Andrew."

"Yeah," Benny said. "This won't be the *first* mystery we've solved."

Grandfather smiled. "You're right about that. You kids have solved a lot of mysteries."

"I have an idea," said Violet. "Let's take the tram tour that Andrew was supposed to be running. Maybe we'll find out something on the tour."

"Good idea," Henry said. "We'll retrace Andrew's steps. Maybe we can learn something about where he was last seen."

They wandered around the exhibits. The information center was busy.

Melanie picked up a microphone and announced the next viewing of the film. Then she added, "The next tram tour leaves in ten minutes. This is a two-hour guided tour. We will end at the observation tower."

One woman fanned herself with a map. "Too hot for me," she said to Jessie. "I think I'll go watch the movie!"

Several people followed the woman into the auditorium. Others went out the door to the tram platform. Melanie came out a few moments later. Her face wore a hurried look.

"You seem short-staffed," said a man as Melanie told them all to board the tram.

The Aldens sat up front, the children sitting in two seats across from one another. Grandfather shared a seat with an older gentleman.

"We *are* short-staffed," Melanie replied, jumping into the driver's seat and clipping a microphone to her shirt collar. "Another ranger came up from Flamingo Visitors' Center to help out these last few days." After checking to see that everyone was safely inside the tram, she started the engine.

In a monotone, she told them about the Shark Valley area. No cars were allowed on the fifteen-mile loop that went deep into the Everglades. But visitors could bike or walk the trail. Most people took the tram, since fifteen miles was a long walk in the summer heat.

"Will we see any alligators?" Benny asked Melanie. He sat directly behind her. "I really, really wish I'd see an alligator."

"You might," she said. "There are lots of alligators in the Everglades." Then she went back to her talk. She told them that nowhere on earth was there a place like the Everglades. The name meant "river of grass." The Everglades began north at Lake Okeechobee, a Native American name meaning "big water." The river flowed south, moving slowly.

"There's a lot of grass in it," Violet said.

"That's called sawgrass," Melanie replied into her microphone. "It only grows here. It's not really grass at all, but a plant called sedge. It's very sharp. Some sawgrass plants are rooted six to fifteen feet deep beneath the water. But here the water is only knee-deep."

The tram stopped several times as Melanie pointed out a white heron, a colorful spoonbill, and other birds.

At last they reached the end of the loop. "If you want," Melanie announced, "you may climb the observation tower. It's sixty-five feet high. You'll be rewarded with a spectacular view of the Everglades."

Benny climbed off the tram with the others. "We didn't see any alligators," he said, disappointed.

"We will," Violet told him. "Maybe it's their nap time." It was very hot. She had brought her camera. It swung around her neck on its strap.

Several older people decided to stay on the shaded tram.

"I'll stay here, too," said Grandfather. "Mr. Austin, here, and I both served in the navy and have a few stories to trade. But you kids go ahead. Be careful."

"We'll watch Benny," Jessie promised.

The observation tower was actually very

safe to climb, with handrails on both sides. Soon they reached the top. The platform had railings all the way around.

"Wow!" Benny cried, running from one side to the other. "We're up as high as the moon!"

Jessie giggled. "Not quite." But the view *was* wonderful, just as Melanie had promised.

"We still don't know anything about Andrew Beldon," said Henry. "I thought we might learn something on the ride."

"I sure hope we find him soon," Jessie said.

Just then Henry pointed to a dark, greenish shape down below. "Look! Is that an alligator?"

"If it is, your wish has come true," Violet told her little brother.

Benny rushed over. "It looks like an old log to me."

"I think alligators *do* look like old logs," Henry told him. "They don't move a lot. But it's pretty far away."

"I'll take a picture," Violet offered. "Just in case it is an alligator."

She stepped forward to position the

greenish log in her viewfinder, then put her finger on the button. Just then someone joggled her arm. Her finger pressed the button, but the camera moved. The picture was spoiled.

She turned to see who had bumped into her. It was a man dressed like a tourist, with a straw hat, a flower-printed shirt, and baggy plaid shorts. He, too, had a camera around his neck. He thumbed through a guidebook on birds.

But as Violet watched him, she realized he wasn't a typical tourist at all. The man wasn't gawking like the others, pointing out birds or other unusual sights. He seemed to be listening to the Aldens. But why? And why did he seem familiar?

She moved away from the man and was about to tell the others.

Just then Benny cried, "Look at that!"

A strange-looking vehicle skimmed quickly over the sawgrass. It was very loud. Birds flew up, wings beating.

"That's an airboat," Henry said. "Maybe we'll get to ride on one."

"They're awfully noisy," said Jessie. "All the birds flew away."

It was time to go back down to the tram. Violet looked around for the strange man, but he had melted into the crowd. When the tram returned to the information center, she thought she glimpsed him hopping quickly off and blending into the swarm of tourists waiting for the next tour.

"We'll look inside once more," said Grandfather. "In case Andrew has come back."

But the ranger at the desk wasn't Andrew. Melanie was getting ready for the next tram tour.

"I don't think we'll get any more information here today," said Grandfather after letting the children buy guidebooks and maps of the Everglades.

"Besides, it's lunchtime," Benny pointed out.

"There aren't any restaurants in the Everglades," Grandfather said. "We'll have to drive back to town."

"I remember a barbecue place on the way in," Henry said.

Sure enough, there was a small barbecue shack on the edge of the Everglades. Everyone piled out of the car and into the restaurant. They ordered iced tea and barbecue platters with extra sauce.

While waiting for their food, the children leafed through their new books.

"We should see all kinds of animals," Henry said excitedly. "Turtles, birds, snakes —"

Jessie shuddered. "No snakes." Normally she was brave, but she didn't like snakes.

"You know what we ought to do?" Henry suggested. "Since we know how to make plaster casts from our trip to upstate New York, we should buy supplies. We want to be prepared if we come across the footprint of a crocodile. Or, if we're very, very lucky, a Florida panther."

"Wildcats?" Benny's eyes grew round. "Here?"

"Not in the restaurant," Jessie teased. "The Florida panther is very rare. I doubt we'll see one. But that's a good idea, Henry."

On the way back to the hotel, the Aldens stopped at a variety store. They loaded up on more bug spray, plaster of paris for making casts, and other supplies.

At the Flamingo, Grandfather went up to his room to make more calls to the Park Service. "This time I'll try Andrew's supervisor," he said.

The kids gathered in the boys' room to discuss the case.

"I think we should try calling Andrew," said Violet. "Maybe he's home by now."

"Great thinking!" Henry praised. After finding Andrew's number in the phone book, he pulled the phone toward him and dialed the number.

"Hello?" answered a woman's voice on the other end.

"Hello," Henry said. "I'm a friend of Andrew Beldon's and I was wondering —"

Click. The line went dead.

Henry held out the receiver. "She hung up on me."

CHAPTER 3

Alligators at Last!

"She hung up?" Jessie echoed.

Violet was looking at the local street map Jessie had brought in with their new books. "Andrew lives at four-oh-two Ancona Lane, apartment three. According to this map, Ancona Lane is only two streets over from this one," she said.

"We can walk there!" Benny said. "And see if Andrew is home."

"He might be sick," Henry added, folding the street map. "He may need help."

First the Aldens went down the hall to let

Grandfather know they were going for a
short walk. He was busy on the phone and
motioned that it was okay for them to leave.

Even though it was hot, the kids ran the
two blocks to Ancona Lane. This street also
had small hotels and houses with rooms
for rent. A VACANCY sign was staked in the
front yard of number 402.

An elderly gentleman sat on the porch
reading a book. He smiled as the kids
climbed the steps.

Henry noticed the front door was closed.
"We're here to see a friend," he said to the
old man. "Do we need to ask permission
from the owner of the house first?"

"I have a key," the old man said, rising.
"I'll let you in. If you know the apartment
number, just go down the hall."

"Thanks," Jessie told him. She pushed
the door open and was greeted by a blast of
cool air and a sour face.

The cool air was welcoming, but the sour
face was not.

"Who are you?" demanded a woman with
red hair.

"We're the Aldens," answered Benny. "We've come to see Andrew Beldon."

The woman's gray eyes narrowed in a frown. "Did you just call on the phone?"

"As a matter of fact, I did —" Henry began.

"Andrew is not here," the woman told him. "And I don't allow kids in my house."

"Thanks for your help," Jessie said. She refused to be impolite.

The door slammed behind them. The old man was still sitting on the porch.

"Old Lady Applegate give you a hard time?" he guessed.

"Yes," said Violet. "Is she always that grouchy?"

"Pretty much. But the lodging is cheap and her cooking isn't too bad." The old man stuck out his hand. "My name is Gus Hummer. Anything I can help you with?"

The children took turns shaking hands and introducing themselves.

"We hope you can," said Jessie. "We're looking for Andrew Beldon. He does live here, doesn't he? In number three?"

"Yep," said Gus. "But Andy's been . . . away for a while."

"Do you know where he is?" asked Henry. "Our grandfather knows Andrew's father. He's trying to find Andrew for his father."

Mr. Hummer opened his mouth, then glanced back at the house. Violet thought she saw a curtain twitch at the window. Was Old Lady Applegate spying on them?

Gus lowered his voice to a hoarse whisper. "The only thing I can say is that Andy is mixed up in something pretty serious. He's disappeared like this before, but never for this long."

"Is Andrew in danger?" Henry prodded.

Gus shook his head. "I don't think so. I think he'll probably show up soon. I can't say any more, kids. But watch out for Old Lady Applegate."

Violet led them across the screened-in porch and down the steps. As soon as they were away from the boardinghouse, they began discussing this new development.

"What could have happened to Andrew?"

asked Jessie. "What would keep him away from his job? And from calling his father?"

"And how does his landlady fit into the picture?" Violet wondered.

"I still think Melanie Harper knows more than she's telling us," said Jessie.

"I'm afraid Andrew is in danger," Henry stated grimly.

The children were silent on the way back to the pink hotel. They went straight to Grandfather's room.

Grandfather was through making calls. "Here's what I've found out," he reported. "Andrew last came to work four days ago, but has not been seen since. Also, his attendance record is spotty."

Benny frowned. "What does that mean?"

"It means Andrew has been arriving at work late, or leaving early, or taking extra time off," said Grandfather. "His supervisor told me Andrew has received two warnings."

"I thought Andrew was responsible," Henry said. "This doesn't sound like him."

"It doesn't," Grandfather agreed. "That's

what's puzzling me. I've known Andy Beldon since he was very young. He was always interested in nature. He was so excited when he became a park ranger. It was a dream come true for him."

"If he loved his job so much, why would he mess it up?" Violet asked.

"Good question." Grandfather looked at them. "You four know something, don't you?"

They told him Andrew lived only two streets over. When they described their visit and what Gus had told them, James Alden drew his brows together.

"Well, it's obvious we won't get any answers from that Applegate woman," he said. "But I don't think we should call the police yet. I don't want to worry Andrew's father."

"I think our best bet is to go back to Shark Valley," Jessie suggested. "I still think Melanie is holding back about Andrew."

"We'll go first thing in the morning," said Grandfather. "It'll be cooler. We'll rent bikes and ride along the trail."

"Oh, boy!" cried Benny. "Maybe we'll see

an alligator!" Then his face fell. "But what'll we do until tomorrow?"

Grandfather pulled out a colorful brochure he had picked up at the airport. "How about a trip to Parrot Jungle?"

"Yippee!" Benny tossed the brochure into the air. "I wish I could live in a jungle when I grow up!"

Everyone had a great time at Parrot Jungle. The park was enormous, with gardens and waterfalls. The birds flew free inside a high, framed net.

"It really *is* a jungle," Violet said. "There are more than twelve hundred varieties of plants here!"

"That's more than I can count," said Benny. He pulled Grandfather toward the stage, where a show was about to begin.

They all laughed at the antics of the colorful parrots, macaws, and cockatoos. The birds cleverly pulled tiny carts or skated on miniature roller skates.

They also saw a flock of flamingos, the tallest of all wading birds. Most of the birds stood on one leg.

"It says here the zookeepers put beets in their food to make them so pink," read Jessie from her guide.

"Yuck!" Benny wrinkled his nose. He'd sure hate to eat beets every day. He tried standing on one leg but fell over, making the others laugh.

"It's hard to keep your balance," said Grandfather. "But I bet you can do something that bird can't."

"What?" said Benny.

"Eat ice cream!"

After hot-fudge sundaes, they discovered the alligator pond. Alligators large and small lay half submerged in the water. Most looked like the greenish log the children had seen from the observation tower.

"Your wish has finally come true," Henry said to Benny. "Can you count all those alligators?"

Benny was disappointed. He wanted to see alligators running around. These alligators were all half asleep.

Jessie understood how he felt. "They're not very exciting, are they?"

"It's okay," Benny said. "I have a new wish now."

Violet nodded. "Zoos are neat, but I'd rather see animals living free, too."

As they walked back to the car, Grandfather said, "It's not always possible for animals to live free. More and more homes and offices are being built on land that animals once lived on. That's why the Florida panther is such a rare animal."

Benny thought about the wild Florida cat as they drove back to the hotel. Wouldn't it be something to see one of *those*? That was his new wish.

The next morning, the Aldens left early. They ate breakfast at the pancake restaurant and headed for Shark Valley. At the park, they rented bicycles and set off down the loop road.

The land was flat, so it was easy riding. But the insects were out in full force. Jessie passed around the bug spray. Even though it was hot, they all wore long sleeves and pants of light cotton.

They stopped several times to look at birds and flowers. Violet took lots of pictures.

Then Benny gave a cry of delight.

"Alligators!" he exclaimed, thrilled. "A whole bunch of them! Out of the water!"

Like people at a beach, a number of alligators were sunning themselves. Although the alligators were far away and not moving, Jessie shuddered.

"Don't worry," Henry reassured her. "They won't hurt us as long as we stay away from them. They only move when threatened or when they're hungry. And they don't eat very often."

"How do we know when they last ate?" Jessie said. She would never like scary reptiles with big sharp teeth, no matter what Henry said.

They decided to bike along a canal. Grandfather had seen a ranger station on the map. Maybe Andrew would be there or someone would know something about him.

But before they reached the ranger station, they came across something they couldn't resist stopping to see.

CHAPTER 4

A New Friend

A girl stood by the roadside, holding a basket. She was a little older than Jessie. Her black hair was in a ponytail with a red ribbon tied around it. She wore a white blouse and a full skirt stitched of many patches — yellow, red, and blue.

"Hello," said the girl. "Welcome to the Miccosukee Village. My name is Irene Osceola."

"Hello," Henry replied. "We were looking for the ranger station."

"It's a little farther down the road," said

Irene. "Won't you come have a cool drink?"

"That's an excellent idea, young lady," said Grandfather.

Benny was puzzled. "Where are we? This isn't the ranger station."

Violet helped him guide his bike to one side. "We're at the Miccosukee Village. Did I say that right, Irene?"

Irene nodded, making her ponytail bounce. "We are one of two tribes who live in the Everglades. Our people live on a reservation in the Glades. Some of us work at the cultural center here. We show tourists how we live and sell our crafts."

Walking behind Irene, Henry read a sign that said, AIRBOAT RIDES, GUIDED TOURS, SNACKS, CRAFTS. TRY OUR FRY BREAD AND PUMPKIN BREAD!

As they followed Irene, the Aldens introduced themselves.

"I'm pleased to know you," said Irene.

Inside the village, tourists examined patchwork vests, skirts, and shirts that were for sale. Others were sipping cold drinks and eating snacks.

"We'll try some of your famous fry bread, too," Grandfather told Irene.

Irene led them to an empty table. "I'll be right back." Soon she returned with cold drinks and slices of warm fried bread.

Violet admired Irene's beautiful skirt. "I love your outfit."

"Thank you." Irene twirled to make the skirt bell. "My mother made it."

"Do you wear those clothes all the time?" Jessie asked.

Irene shook her head. "Not always. I wear jeans and T-shirts, too."

"Tell us about your tribe," Grandfather urged. "By the way, the bread is delicious."

"Thank you," said Irene. "Our tribe has lived in the Everglades for more than a hundred years. We raise pumpkins, squash, and corn. I travel to school on my father's airboat."

"Neat!" said Benny. Ever since he'd seen one of the noisy boats skimming over the grass, he'd wanted to ride on one.

Irene laughed. "Well, it's the only way to get to school!"

"What are those buildings called?" asked Henry.

"Chickees," Irene replied. "Those are our traditional dwellings. We sleep in hammocks or up on cypress platforms."

"It's like a tree house," Violet commented.

"We also have other houses," Irene added. "With screened windows all around and shutters that can be closed during storms and hurricanes."

Benny wiped his mouth and declared, "I want to live here."

"We'd love to have you, Benny," Irene said. "But you might get tired of living outdoors."

Benny shook his head. "No, we used to do it all the time."

Violet explained that the Aldens had once lived in an abandoned boxcar. "That was before Grandfather found us," she concluded.

Irene seemed impressed. "You've had very exciting lives."

"We solve mysteries, too," Benny added.

"But we're stumped on our current case," Jessie said, her chin on her fist.

Irene leaned forward, fascinated. "You solve mysteries! I love to read mystery stories. Tell me about your case."

This time Grandfather answered. "Maybe you can help us, Irene. We're looking for a missing park ranger. His name is Andrew Beldon."

Irene's dark eyes widened. "Ranger Beldon! I know him well. He brings me books from the big public library. We have very few books on the reservation. Ranger Beldon stops by the library every two weeks."

"When did you see him last?" Henry asked.

"Let me see." Irene thought a moment. "It's been more than two weeks. He picked up my books and returned them to the big library. But he hasn't been back. I was wondering why we hadn't seen him lately."

"No one has seen him for a while," said Violet. Then she explained how Grandfather's friend had asked him to come look for Andrew.

"That's very strange," Irene agreed. "Ranger Beldon loves his job. He wouldn't just quit."

"I've talked to officials at the Park Service," said Grandfather, "but they don't know where he is, either."

"If Ranger Beldon is lost in the Glades, he could be in real trouble," Irene said.

"That's what we're afraid of," said Henry.

James Alden pointed to the sign. "I see airboat tours are given here."

Irene nodded eagerly. "My father, Billy Osceola, has his own airboat. He often drives tourists into the Glades."

"Can we ride on your father's airboat to look for Andrew Beldon?" Benny asked. "Maybe we'll find him that way."

Now Irene frowned. "Tourists like the airboats because they're exciting. But they are very noisy. The big motors scare the birds and animals." Then she brightened. "But we can look for Ranger Beldon by canoe! Canoes are quiet and safe. We can go almost anywhere in them. Places you can't get to on foot or by bike."

The canoes were all rented, so Grandfather rented three canoes for the next day. They bade Irene good-bye.

Back on their bikes, the Aldens peddled away from the Miccosukee Village to the ranger station. But no one there had heard from or seen Andrew Beldon in several days. The Everglades National Park had many employees and a dozen visitors' centers — plus there were feeding stations for wildlife and campsites. Andrew could be anywhere.

Grandfather and the children were hot and tired when they returned the bicycles to the Shark Valley entrance. They went inside the visitors' center to cool off. The boys looked for the water fountain.

Violet and Jessie walked to the front desk. When Melanie Harper saw Jessie and Violet, she frowned.

Jessie strode up to the desk. "Hi," she said cheerfully. "Remember me? Jessie Alden?"

Melanie's glance was far from welcoming. "You and your family still looking for An-

drew Beldon? He hasn't come in to work."

"Has he called or anything?" Violet pressed.

"Nope." Melanie didn't seem the least bit concerned. In fact, Jessie thought, Melanie was a little *too* unconcerned. It almost seemed like an act.

Jessie believed the girl was hiding something. "Do you have any idea where Andrew went? Or why he hasn't come back to work? It's just not like him to quit without telling anybody."

"Do you know what I think?" Melanie said, leaning forward confidentially.

"What?" Jessie's heart beat faster.

"I think Andrew has let his obsession go too far this time."

"His what?" asked Violet.

But then a flock of tourists breezed through the door. Melanie greeted them with a bright smile and an Everglades map.

Jessie knew the Park Service woman wouldn't say any more to them.

Henry and Benny came over.

"What's up?" Henry wanted to know.

"We've been talking to Melanie," Violet replied. "She said something strange about Andrew."

"What?" asked Henry.

Jessie filled him in. "Melanie said she thought Andrew had let his obsession go too far this time and that's why he's disappeared."

"Ob-session?" Benny said. "What does that mean?"

"It means that Andrew has been really interested in something that takes up all his time," Henry replied. "You know what I think, though?" Henry added. "Melanie is after Andrew's job. She's always here at the visitors' center."

"She complained about having to do his work and hers, too," said Violet. "I bet Henry's right. Melanie wants everyone to know she's working so hard, so she'll get Andrew's job when he comes back."

Jessie had been thinking. "Melanie could be jealous."

"Of what?" asked Violet.

"Maybe he and Melanie were boyfriend

and girlfriend. Maybe Andrew broke up with her. He could have met another girl he liked better," Jessie said.

Henry understood where Jessie was going. "And Melanie didn't like it, so she's doing everything she can to make him look bad."

Grandfather came up just then. "It's so hot. Why don't we go to a movie to cool off? We'll have an early supper and be all ready for our canoe trip tomorrow."

"Good idea." Benny swung Grandfather's hand as they left the center. "Can we have key lime pie today?"

"Do you know what that is?" asked Grandfather with a smile.

"No, but it's something everybody has here," said Benny. Any kind of pie was fine with him.

The last out the door, Jessie turned to glance back at the front desk.

Melanie Harper was watching them. Her blue eyes were secretive.

Jessie was certain Melanie knew something she wasn't telling.

CHAPTER 5

A Clue in the Muck

Irene Osceola was waiting for the Aldens when they pulled into the Miccosukee Village the next morning.

"The canoe ramp is this way," she said. Today she wore jeans, a long-sleeved T-shirt, and sneakers.

"It's good you all wore pants and long sleeves," she said as they approached the landing. "It's very buggy in the Glades."

"We're practically coated with insect spray," Jessie said. "Plus we brought along extra, just in case." She held up a pack that contained water, sunscreen, insect repellent, and other supplies.

Three lightweight fiberglass canoes bobbed in the water at the dock. The canoes looked odd, Henry thought. These were nearly flat-bottomed and wider than canoes he had paddled on lakes.

"Our people used to make dugout cypress canoes," Irene explained, "but we have to conserve the cypress trees." She grinned. "Also, these are easier to handle."

Grandfather assigned the canoes. "I'll take one with Benny. Irene, you go with Jessie. And Henry will take the third one with Violet."

Henry was looking around. "Where are the oars?"

Irene giggled. "No oars. We don't sit down and paddle these canoes. The sawgrass and lily pads are too thick. We stand up and pole the canoes through the water."

"Well, I'm game," said Grandfather, stepping into a canoe. He helped Benny in, then took the pack Jessie handed him.

The others climbed into their canoes and

found poles in the bottoms. Irene untied the ropes and hopped into her canoe.

"Stand at each end," she instructed them, poling her and Jessie's canoe away from the dock first. "These boats won't tip over easily, but it'll take you a while to get used to poling instead of paddling."

"We aren't going anywhere!" Benny called back to Grandfather.

"That's because we're not poling in the same direction," Grandfather said, laughing. "I'm trying to push the canoe forward and you're making it go backward!"

Irene came alongside their canoe and gave them a push. "Now you've got it, Benny! You guys are doing great."

As the three canoes moved slowly downriver, Irene explained that they were heading west into the "river of grass."

"Why are we going this way?" Henry asked Irene.

"This is where I see Ranger Beldon a lot," Irene answered. "He has his own canoe."

"Apparently he hasn't been to work in the last several days," Grandfather said. He and

Benny were finally catching up to the others. "Do you think he might have come into the Everglades alone and is lost?"

"It's possible," Irene said. "Ranger Beldon knows the Glades pretty well. But there are still places no one has ever seen, so even someone who knows the hidden places can get lost."

Jessie remembered what Melanie Harper had said. "Do you know anything about an 'obsession' Andrew has?"

Irene wrinkled her brow under her baseball cap. "I'm not sure. Maybe the Florida panther," Irene said.

"Panthers!" Benny said with awe. "Those big wildcats?"

"Yes," said Irene. "Not too many people know about our wildcats."

"We read about panthers in our nature book," said Violet. "They only live in the Everglades, right?"

"Which are shrinking every day," Irene said, shaking her head sadly. "Hear the cars? We aren't very far from the highway. That highway and the canals men dug to drain the swamp have made the Glades smaller. Houses and stores and farms steal land from the Everglades."

"And less land means fewer homes for animals and birds," Grandfather put in. "That's why the Everglades National Park is here, to protect and preserve what's left."

Henry wanted to get back to the missing ranger. "You say Andrew Beldon is interested in the Florida panthers?"

"Ranger Beldon worries about the panthers. He's afraid they will disappear altogether. It's happened before — other animals have become extinct," said Irene. "Crocodiles are also very endangered."

Benny glanced excitedly around the still water. "There are crocodiles in here?"

"Very, very few," Irene informed him. "It's rare to see a crocodile and even rarer to see a panther. My family is of the Panther Clan. The Miccosukee belong to different family clans, like the Bird, Wind, or Otter Clans. We members of the Panther Clan understand the beauty of the panther. Ranger Beldon does, too."

Just then they came upon a small island. White herons stood in the shallow water near the island, stalking small fish and frogs.

The trees that grew on the island were the strangest Benny had ever seen. One tree seemed to stand up on two legs out of the water.

"Those trees look like people!" he exclaimed.

"My ancestors thought so, too," Irene told him with a smile. "They are mangrove trees. My people called them 'the walking trees.' The roots are like legs."

Then she explained that the island wasn't really an island, but a "hammock." A tree would take root. Seeds drifting downstream would cling to the mangrove's roots. Over the years, dirt gathered and more plants and trees grew until a humped mound rose out of the water.

They poled close to the mangrove hammock. Violet stopped to take pictures of wild orchids growing right on the sides of the trees.

"Oh, look!" Jessie declared. She pointed

to a colorful snail on a tree. The conical shell swirled in shades of gray, blue, beige, and lavender.

Bullfrogs leaped among the lily pads. Bottle-green dragonflies skimmed over the surface. A harmless water snake swam between Henry's and Irene's canoes. Benny could hardly keep still. He didn't want to miss anything.

Grandfather took his hat off to swat at the mosquitoes. "You're never alone here, are you?" he joked.

"Not for a second," Irene agreed. "Though sometimes your companion is too small to see!"

As long as they kept moving, the insects weren't too bad. Irene had told them to expect bugs, but Jessie couldn't believe the dense clouds of mosquitoes and tiny no-see-ums.

"Is this a place Andrew might stop?" Henry asked Irene.

She nodded. "Since he came this way, he probably stopped here often. Ranger Beldon was always looking for any sign of a panther."

"Have you ever seen one?" Benny asked, awed that wildcats could be lurking in the tangle of undergrowth.

Irene shook her head. "People look for years and never see a panther. My father saw one once, when he was a little boy about your age, Benny. But only that one time."

"Let's tie up our canoes and walk around," Grandfather suggested. "Maybe we'll see some sign that Andrew has been here."

Irene directed them to a mangrove tree with extra-long roots. They tied up their canoes and waded in the shallow water to the hammock.

"The water is so warm," Violet remarked. "I could take a bath in it!"

"That's because it's summer," said Irene. "In the winter and during the rainy season in the spring, the water is cooler."

Benny scrambled up the side of the hammock, using a vine like a rope. "This place is neat!"

It took the others longer to make their

way through the Caribbean pines, saw palmettos, and live oaks. Henry was amazed at the variety of ferns growing right in the bark on the trees. The Everglades was a truly magical place.

"What is this?" he asked Irene, pointing to a plant with yellow and orange flowers.

"We call that *coontie*," Irene replied. "We grate the root and make flour after it's dry. Then we add water and make a kind of cereal, *sofkee*. It's really good."

Jessie looked up at the sky and watched a huge bird lazily circle overhead. The bird could see a lot better than they could. *Where is Andrew Beldon?* she asked the bird silently.

Then she thought of something.

"Irene," she began, "do you know a ranger named Melanie Harper?"

Irene frowned slightly. "A little. She's blond and pretty, isn't she? I think she and Andrew were dating."

"That's what I thought," Jessie said. "But whenever we talk to Melanie, she acts as if she doesn't care about Andrew at all."

"They are not really friends anymore," Irene said. "Andrew came to the village one day with my books. He looked sad and I asked him what was wrong. He told me about what had happened with Melanie Harper."

Not paying attention to where she was going, Violet tripped over a mangrove root. She caught herself before she fell. Then she saw it.

"Hey, guys!" she cried. "Look at this!"

In the soft, squishy mud was part of a shoe print.

Grandfather leaned over. "Good work, Violet. That's the heel of somebody's boot."

Benny poked his finger into the spongy mud. "What is this stuff?"

"It's called muck," Irene said. "Sometimes the muck can be dangerous if you fall into it. It's hard to climb out."

"This might be a clue," Henry stated. "Jessie, did you bring our casting kit?"

"Right in the pack," she replied, digging out the small sack of plaster of paris, a tin dish, a jar of petroleum jelly, and a metal ring.

Benny got water to mix the plaster in the tin dish while Violet greased the inside of the metal ring with the petroleum jelly.

Irene watched in fascination. "You are like real detectives," she said as Jessie carefully placed the ring around the print.

"We've done this before," Jessie said. "On another mystery case."

Henry stirred the plaster until it was thick. Then he poured it over the ring, covering the heel print. "This stuff dries pretty fast," he said.

They waited until the plaster had set, then Violet lifted the ring with a perfect cast of the print inside.

She stared at it. "That's odd," she said. "There's a mark like a V on the sole."

"A clue," Benny declared. "Maybe this is Andrew's shoe print. We might be on his trail!"

Violet gazed into the wild, noisy Everglades. She hoped Benny was right.

CHAPTER 6

More Secrets

By the time the plaster cast was dry, Grandfather decided it was time to get out of the midday heat.

They all climbed into their canoes and poled back to the Miccosukee Village.

"Thanks for your help," Henry said to Irene as they walked up the dock. "We wouldn't have found that print on our own."

"Glad I could help," she said. "Ranger Beldon is a good friend. I hope you find him soon."

Jessie came up just then. "Grandfather says we're stopping at the information center, since it's on the way back to the hotel. Thanks, Irene. You were a great guide."

Irene walked the Aldens to their rental car and waved as they drove down Route Forty-one.

"If no one has heard from Andy today, I'm going to speak to the head of the Park Service down here," Grandfather said, pulling into the parking lot of Shark Valley.

"At least we have one clue," said Benny. He held the odd-looking plaster print in his lap.

"Maybe," Violet said. "This heel print might not have anything to do with Andrew's disappearance. It could belong to any tourist who stopped to explore, like we did."

"You could be right," said Benny. But deep inside he felt the heel cast was part of the mystery.

For once, the information center wasn't very busy. Melanie Harper was at the front desk, straightening a stack of maps.

Her face showed she recognized the

Aldens, but Jessie couldn't read any expression. She couldn't tell if Melanie was glad or irritated to see them.

"Before you ask," Melanie said, "we heard from Andrew. He called in about an hour ago."

Grandfather sighed with relief. "That's wonderful! Where is he?"

"He's sick," Melanie replied, dusting the counter with a rag. "He won't be back for a while."

"Sick?" queried Henry. "What's wrong with him? How long will he be out?"

Melanie shrugged. "He didn't say and I didn't ask. I've been doing both Andrew's and my work for almost a week now. Our supervisor has noticed what a good job I'm doing." She smiled smugly. "I'll probably get a promotion!"

"So you're saying Andrew won't have a job when he comes back to work?" Jessie asked. She didn't like Melanie's tone. The other ranger acted as if she was *glad* Andrew was sick.

"Oh, he'll have a job," Melanie replied.

"But not *this* job." She picked up the microphone and announced briskly that the film would start in five minutes. It was clear she wasn't going to talk to the Aldens anymore.

The few tourists wandering around inside headed for the door. The Aldens followed. Outside, it seemed hotter than ever.

In the parking lot, they were amazed to see an enormous alligator stretched out. He yawned mightily, showing several rows of pointed teeth.

"Wow!" cried Benny. "Look at that!"

Violet snapped several pictures from a safe distance.

Henry gave a low whistle. "I bet he's at least nine feet long!"

"Can we go now?" Jessie said nervously. She didn't like alligators in parking lots. They were scary enough in the water.

Grandfather opened the car door for her. "I'm not crazy about them, either," he said to her. "Besides, the alligator was taking up two parking spots!"

Giggling, Jessie hugged him, then

climbed into the front seat. Grandfather always knew the right thing to say!

Next they had to find a place for lunch.

"Any suggestions?" Grandfather asked.

"How about that barbecue place near here?" said Violet.

"The barbecue place it is," said Grandfather.

Minutes later they arrived at the red wooden building. They were the only customers, so service was fast.

Soon they were eating chicken sandwiches, french fries, and corn on the cob, washed down with sweetened iced tea. It had been a long morning. No one said much until the waitress brought another pitcher of iced tea.

Refreshed and full, they discussed the mystery.

"If Andrew's been sick all this time," began Violet, "why didn't he tell anybody? Why didn't he at least call his father?"

"Maybe he was too sick," said Benny.

Grandfather squeezed lemon into his glass of iced tea. "Benny has a good point.

Andrew might have been too ill to pick up the phone and call before today."

"Then why didn't his landlady say so?" Jessie asked. "We were there and she never told us Andrew was sick. She wouldn't tell us anything!"

"Except to go away," Benny said.

"He could be sick someplace besides the rooming house," Henry put in. "But that doesn't seem very likely."

"I think Melanie acted weird," Violet said. "She seemed happy Andrew was out sick!"

Jessie nodded her agreement. "We need to watch her. I think she might be the key to this mystery."

"Maybe the mystery is over," said Grandfather. "I'll call Andrew when we get back to our hotel. If he's just been out sick, I'll call his father and tell him so."

"And then we'll go back home?" Benny asked. He wasn't ready to leave Florida yet. He had gotten his first wish — to see alligators. But now he had a second, even better wish.

"We'll see." Grandfather smiled. "Let's head back to the hotel, okay?"

On the drive back, Jessie was thinking about Melanie. Was it possible that Andrew had called in before and Melanie had taken the call? Maybe Melanie had *pretended* she hadn't heard from him, so she could get his job.

At the Flamingo Hotel, Mrs. Johnson waved a pink slip at Grandfather.

Everything about the hotel was pink, thought Violet. Even the notepaper.

"Message for you, Mr. Alden. A man called this morning right after you left. It sounded pretty urgent. He'd like you to call him back right away." Mrs. Johnson left the hall.

Grandfather looked at the paper. "It's from Tom Beldon. He wants to know what I've learned about his son. I don't want him to be upset, especially since we've been out of touch for several days. I'll call him now, before I check on Andrew."

He went upstairs.

Jessie looked at Henry. "You know what?

While Grandfather is on the phone with Mr. Beldon, we could go to Andrew's rooming house and see him in person!"

"Great idea, Jessie," said Violet. "Grandfather doesn't mind if we walk around the block."

"Or two blocks." Henry was already out the door.

The others quickly caught up with him. A cool breeze stirred the royal palms. The sky was dark in the west. A storm was brewing.

By the time they reached Old Lady Applegate's boardinghouse, fat drops of rain had begun to fall.

Gus wasn't sitting on the screened-in porch, but the swing was moving slightly as if he had just gone inside.

Jessie knocked on the front door.

After a moment, the door opened a crack. An eye peered out. "What do you kids want?" The gruff voice undoubtedly belonged to the landlady, Old Lady Applegate.

"To see Andrew Beldon," Henry spoke up. "We heard he was sick."

"Yeah," added Benny. "We came to cheer him up."

"He's not here," said the landlady.

"That's impossible," said Violet. "We just heard that Andrew is sick. Where else would he be?"

The door opened inward so fast, Jessie nearly fell over.

"All right," said Old Lady Applegate ungraciously. "You don't believe me — see for yourself. Andrew Beldon's room is the second door on the left. Don't touch anything!"

"We won't," Henry promised. "We just want to visit him."

The kids filed down the hall. Andrew's door was closed. The landlady unlocked it with a ring of keys. She stood behind them to make sure they didn't go inside.

Benny noticed the panther poster on the wall right away. He'd like to have one like it. Andrew's room was fairly neat. The bed was made. His books were stacked by size in a bookcase. No shoes or clothes littered the floor.

"Now do you believe me?" Old Lady Applegate demanded. "If Andrew Beldon is sick, he's obviously staying someplace else. He's behind in his rent, too. If he doesn't pay up by the end of the week, I'm renting his room to someone else."

"What will happen to Andrew's things?" Violet asked. She had noticed the photographs on Andrew's desk.

The landlady shrugged. "I'll box them up and store them. If Andrew doesn't claim his stuff soon, then I guess it's mine."

Henry leaned inside the doorway just a little. Along the wall, behind the door, was a dresser. One drawer was pulled out and socks hung untidily over the edge.

"You can see Andrew is not here," the landlady said, clearly flustered. She pulled the door shut hastily.

Henry wondered if she had something to hide. Did everyone connected with Andrew Beldon have a secret?

"Yes," said Violet. "We'll leave now."

Outside, the rain shower had passed already. Steam rose from the sidewalk.

Violet asked the others, "Did you guys see all the panther books in Andrew's bookcase?"

"And that neat poster?" added Benny. "Rrrr!"

"Melanie was right about one thing: Andrew is definitely obsessed with the Florida panther," Jessie stated. She shook her head. "But Andrew's room looked as if he hadn't been there in days."

"I saw something, too," said Henry. "A moldy piece of bread sitting on the table. It takes several days for mold to grow, and I bet if he'd been here he would have thrown it away."

"Why would he leave all his things?" Violet wondered. "He has some very nice books and pictures."

"I don't know," Jessie answered. "But I think we ought to learn about the Florida panther. If it's Andrew's obsession, it should be ours, too. At least until we find him."

Henry tapped the side of his head. "Good idea, Jessie. If we want to find Andrew, we have to think like him!"

CHAPTER 7

Wildcats and Radios

The next morning, they all piled into the rental car and drove south to the main visitors' center in the Everglades.

"I can't believe the runaround we're getting," Grandfather said as he waved his pass at the ranger in the booth. "First Melanie Harper says she heard that Andrew was sick. And then you children go to Andrew's boardinghouse and find out he's not there!"

"If I wasn't feeling well, I'd want to be home," said Violet.

Henry said, "We can't really blame the

park people. They've been helpful, except for Melanie. I hope Andrew's father wasn't too upset when you told him you hadn't found his son yet."

Pulling into an empty parking space, Grandfather sighed. "I'm afraid he did become upset. He hasn't heard from Andrew in almost three weeks, but I told him to wait a little longer before he calls the police."

"We'll get clues when we find out about the panther," Benny said confidently.

The main visitors' center was busy. Several park rangers were on duty, handing out brochures and maps, directing people to the various walking trails, and announcing guided hikes.

"We want to learn about the Florida panther," said Jessie, walking up to the main desk. "Can someone tell us about them?"

The young man behind the counter replied, "Actually, one of our panther experts happens to be on duty in the Royal Palms Visitors' Center. That's just next door. Ask for Nelda."

"Thanks!" Jessie said. Not all rangers

were like Melanie Harper. This one was really nice.

And so was Nelda Pearson, as her name badge read. She was describing an easy boardwalk trail to a group of Canadians. When she finished with them, she saw Grandfather and the children.

"How may I help you?" Nelda asked.

"One of your coworkers from the main center told us you are an expert on the Florida panther," said Grandfather. "I'm James Alden. My grandchildren and I are particularly interested in this animal."

Nelda glanced at her watch. "You're in luck. My break is coming up. How about if we walk the Gumbo Lingo Trail."

They all went outside to a well-marked path. "This is the entrance to the Gumbo Lingo Trail. It's named after the gumbo lingo trees you'll see."

At first the Aldens were too busy looking at the scenery to talk. Besides the odd-named gumbo lingo trees, there were more royal palms, colorful birds flying overhead, and orchids growing wild.

Then Henry remembered their mission. "Do you know Andrew Beldon?"

Nelda stopped and stared at him. "Andy! Yes, we've worked together for years. But I haven't seen him lately."

"Neither has anyone else. And his father hasn't heard from him in quite a while," Jessie said. "Mr. Beldon asked Grandfather to come down here and find Andrew."

"He's usually assigned to the Shark Valley Center," Nelda said.

"He hasn't been to work in days," Benny put in. "A lady told us he was sick, but we still can't find him."

"Benny means Melanie Harper," Violet supplied. "Melanie is doing both her job and Andrew's. She told us yesterday Andrew had called in sick."

Jessie picked up the story. "But we went to Andrew's boardinghouse and he wasn't there. We've heard that Andrew is interested in the Florida panther. Maybe if we knew more about them, it would help us find Andrew."

"Boy," Nelda said, almost to herself. "I

hope Andrew isn't in trouble." Louder she said, "Andrew and I work together a lot with the big cats. He's afraid they'll become extinct."

"Are they that rare?" Violet asked.

Nelda's cheerful voice became somber. "There are no more than thirty to fifty Florida panthers left in the wild. Probably closer to thirty."

"What happened to them?" Benny asked.

Nelda waved an arm. "The Everglades is their home. But the Glades are much smaller than they used to be. As more people moved in, that made less space for the big cats. They need lots of territory to hunt and live in."

"I've heard that some are killed by cars," Grandfather said.

Nelda nodded. "And hunters. The Florida panther was only given federal protection in nineteen fifty-eight. Now it's an endangered species. They live deep in the Glades."

"We keep hearing they are hard to see," Henry said. "If a panther is so hard to spot, how do you keep track of them?"

"We use electronic collars," Nelda explained. "We track the cats — they do leave signs, like paw prints or tufts of hair. Then we give the animals something to make them sleepy. While they are asleep, we treat them for illnesses or injuries and then put an electronic radio collar around their necks. Then we let the cats go. Now we're able to keep tabs on them."

Benny was confused. "Watch has a collar. It doesn't have a radio on it."

"Watch is our dog back home in Connecticut," Violet told Nelda. "I'm confused, too. How does the collar work?"

"Each collar is a transmitter," Nelda said, speaking more slowly so Benny could understand. "The collar sends out high-pitched beeps or signals. We can hear those beeps on special equipment we have."

"How do you know one cat from another?" Henry asked. He knew a little about radio electronics.

"Good question. Each cat is assigned a number and its personal signal. For example, Cat Number Three has a special frequency. When we tune in our transmitters and hear that signal, we know we're picking up Cat Number Three's movements."

"And that signal tells you where Cat Number Three is?" asked Grandfather.

"It tells us what area she's in," Nelda said. "If she's not moving, we can get an even better idea of where she is."

Jessie shook her head. "It's so complicated! Don't the cats mind wearing those collars?"

"At first they do, but then they get used to them," Nelda said. "It's the only way we can help them survive in the wild. Andrew has followed more cats than any of us. He monitors them day and night sometimes."

Violet had an idea. "Do you think that's where Andrew might be now? Following one of the cats?"

"He could be," Nelda replied. "But it would be foolish for Andrew to go into the Glades alone, especially if one of the big cats was hurt. Andrew could be injured himself. No one would know where he is."

The Aldens were quiet for a moment.

"Couldn't Andrew call you on his radio?" Jessie asked Nelda.

"Yes, he could," Nelda replied reluctantly. "I've tried calling *him*, but I don't get a reply."

Henry remembered what Gus Hummer, the old man who lived in Andrew's boardinghouse, had said. He thought that Andrew was mixed up in "something pretty serious." Could it have to do with the Florida panthers? Maybe Gus Hummer knew more than he was telling.

"We should start back," Nelda said suddenly. "My break is over, and we're very busy today."

"There are a lot of tourists here," Grandfather noted. "I'm surprised, since it's summer. I would think people wouldn't want to tour the Everglades in this heat."

Nelda led the way back down the Gumbo Lingo Trail. "The Glades are popular year-round. After Yellowstone, the Everglades is the second-largest national park."

Back at the Royal Palms Visitors' Center, the Aldens thanked Nelda for her time and information. Once again, she appeared concerned.

"If you hear anything at all about Andrew, please let me know. And if I hear from him, I'll be sure to tell you," she promised, jotting her phone number on a piece of paper.

Jessie took the paper and tucked it in her pocket. On another piece of paper, Jessie wrote the address and phone number of the Flamingo Hotel and handed it to Nelda. "You can reach us here. You've been a big help. Thanks again."

Benny had discovered the postcard rack. He was looking for one with a picture of a Florida panther. It would be fun to send it to Watch and Mrs. McGregor. The children could each write something in the small square —

He stopped, postcard in midair, and looked down. He saw shoes on the other side of the postcard rack. Thick-soled boots with orange laces. The boots clumped away and disappeared around the corner.

But not before Benny caught a glimpse of

bushy hair tucked under a squashed felt hat. He didn't remember the hat, but the hair looked familiar. Where had he seen that man before?

Grandfather came up and said, "We're stopping to talk to Irene on the way home. Maybe she's heard something about Andrew."

"Oh, boy!" Benny cried. "Can I have some pumpkin bread?"

"We'll all have a snack," Grandfather said. He purchased Benny's postcard and they left.

It was a long drive north to the Miccosukee Village. The children discussed what Nelda had said.

"If Andrew went into the Glades to rescue a cat, why wouldn't he tell her?" Jessie pointed out. "They work together."

"This mystery gets more and more mysterious," Benny declared.

"I hope Andrew has enough supplies," said Grandfather. "If he's in the Glades without food and water, he could be in more trouble than any panther!"

When they pulled into the Miccosukee Village, Irene ran up to their car.

"I have news!" she said breathlessly.

The children climbed quickly out of the car.

"What is it?" Jessie asked, her heart in her throat.

"My father — he gives airboat tours — anyway, he believes he saw Ranger Beldon last night!" Irene's dark eyes glittered with excitement.

"Did your father talk to him?" asked Grandfather.

Irene shook her head. "My father called out Andrew's name, but the man ran and hid. That's very strange because my father and Ranger Beldon are friends."

"That *is* weird," Violet agreed. "If the man wasn't Andrew, then who was he? And if it *was* Andrew, he obviously doesn't want to be found."

Benny was right. The mystery *was* getting more and more mysterious.

CHAPTER 8

A Visitor Brings a Clue

"Is your father here?" asked Henry.

Irene nodded, her ponytail bouncing.

"Can we talk to him?" Henry asked.

"He's fixing a friend's airboat," she said. "I'll take you over to him."

The ramp had two airboats docked. Jessie figured one belonged to Irene's father.

"Daddy," said Irene, "these are the people I told you about. The ones trying to find Ranger Beldon?"

A big man wiped his hands on a rag and

came over. He shook hands with Grandfather.

"Billy Osceola," he said. "Nice to meet you."

"James Alden," said Grandfather in return. "Glad to meet you, Mr. Osceola. These are my grandchildren, Henry, Jessie, Violet, and Benny."

"Irene said you saw a man in the Glades last night," Henry said. "Do you know who he was?"

Mr. Osceola shook his head. "He looked like Andrew Beldon. But when I called out to him, he ran away."

Violet looked up at Mr. Osceola. "Why would he have run away?"

"I don't know. I just hope he's okay." Irene's father was grave. "It's easy to become lost in the backwaters of the Glades."

"Do you think Andrew is lost?" asked Jessie. All along, she was afraid this might be true.

Mr. Osceola shrugged. "I doubt it. Andrew Beldon knows many secret places of the Glades. That's probably why no one has found him. He can be as quiet as the panther he likes so much."

"Can you take us to where you saw this man?" Grandfather asked Mr. Osceola.

"Yes," Irene's father replied. "But it's not a short trip. I think you should count on spending the night."

"How can I do that?" asked Grandfather.

"The park has a chickee built nearby," said Mr. Osceola. "They have several around the park for people who want to camp out overnight. But they are primitive. Bring everything you need with you. Irene and I will come, too. And you'll need to get a permit from the ranger station."

"I can do that now," said Grandfather. "The station is just down the road."

"Are we going to take canoes?" Henry asked. If the place was as far as Mr. Osceola said, poling a canoe would take them forever.

"I'll take you in my airboat," Irene's father replied. "I can drop you off in the morning and come back later."

"We're going to ride in one of those?"

Benny cried, jumping up and down on the dock. "Yippee!"

Mr. Osceola smiled. "Yes, airboats are fun to ride in. They are very fast."

"I like to go fast!" Benny said. "Almost as much as I like to eat."

Everyone laughed.

"Okay, Benny," said Violet. "Let's go to the snack bar for some pumpkin bread."

"I'll join you later," said Grandfather. "I want to discuss the details with Mr. Osceola and then drive to the ranger station for our camping permit."

The snack bar wasn't crowded. The children purchased thick slices of pumpkin bread and cold drinks. They all sat at an empty table.

"You are in for a real experience," Irene told them. "Not many people go where you are going tomorrow."

"I'm glad you'll be with us," said Violet. "I'm a little nervous."

"Don't be," Irene reassured her. "A chickee is very safe. You can bring sleeping bags if you want. I'll bring along hammocks, too."

"I want to sleep in a hammock," Benny declared. He couldn't wait to start this adventure.

A tour bus stopped out front. Irene had to leave the Aldens to wait on customers.

Henry picked up his trash. "I think we should go. Grandfather is probably waiting for us outside."

He pushed his chair back. As he did, a man just behind him poured his drink down Henry's back!

Instead of apologizing, the man muttered, "Why don't you look where you're going!" Then he hustled away.

Jessie grabbed a handful of napkins and dabbed at Henry's shirt.

"It's okay," Henry said. "One minute in the sun and I'll be dry."

Violet stared at the rude man's bushy hair. "I know that man! He was on top of the observation tower. He made me mess up my picture."

"I've seen him, too," Benny said. "Today, when I was looking at postcards."

"And he was at the house at the end of

our street," Jessie added. "The first evening when we took a walk. Remember?"

Henry frowned. "Why would the same man always be in the same places we are?"

"Coincidence, maybe?" Jessie suggested.

"I don't think so." But before Henry could say more, Grandfather came in.

"We should leave," he told them. "We have a lot of supplies to buy for our camp-out."

The rest of the afternoon was spent buying sleeping bags, more insect repellent, cookware, food, a lantern, mosquito netting, and utensils.

"We have a lot of this stuff at home," Jessie remarked as they loaded the bulky sacks into the trunk of their car.

"Yes, but our old sleeping bags are getting a little worn out," Grandfather said.

"Can we keep the old ones in our boxcar?" Benny asked. "For sleepovers?"

"Good idea." Grandfather rumpled Benny's hair. "Although after tomorrow night, you might not want to camp out again for a while."

"Why? What's going to happen tomorrow?" Jessie asked. "Irene told us the Glades are noisy at night."

"Mr. Osceola told me the same thing," Grandfather said. "I just think none of us will get much sleep, that's all. There's nothing to be afraid of or we wouldn't go. According to Irene's father, the place where he saw the man who looked like Andy is deep in the Glades."

"And we'll have to search for him," Henry added. "So we can't make this trip all in one day."

"Exactly." Grandfather got behind the wheel. "Let's go back to the hotel and think about where we want to eat dinner."

But the children were too excited to eat when they reached the pink hotel. This time tomorrow they would be deep in the Everglades. Anything could happen!

They sat out on the porch and signed Benny's postcard.

To their surprise, an old man came up the walk. It was Gus Hummer.

"Mr. Hummer!" Jessie said, getting up to

give him her seat on the glider. "Did you come to see us?"

"I did indeed. Just let me catch my breath." The old man sat down and took a few shaky breaths. "It's farther over here than I thought!"

"You should have called us," said Violet. "You could have left a message with Mrs. Johnson. We would have come over to your house. Can I get you a drink?"

"Water would be fine," said Gus.

Violet came back moments later with a pitcher of ice water on a tray and several glasses. Gus drank an entire glass, set it on the tray, and wiped his mouth with his handkerchief.

"I had to come over here," he told the Aldens. "I can't talk freely at my boarding-house."

"Why not?" asked Benny.

"Because Old Lady Applegate eavesdrops. That woman is always listening at doors. She hears everything!" Gus remarked.

Henry poured their guest a second glass of cold water. "What do you want to tell us? Does it have to do with Andrew?"

Gus nodded. "Old Lady Applegate was snooping in Andrew's room. He hasn't been back in days, you know."

"Yes, we know," put in Jessie. "Do you think the landlady took something from Andrew's room?"

Gus waved a hand. "She takes things from all our rooms. Little things, like pocket change, knickknacks. She once took a picture of my late wife. I think she sold the frame. I wouldn't have minded so much if she'd left the picture."

"That's terrible!" Violet cried. "Did you tell the police?"

"I didn't have any proof. It would be her word against the word of an old man," Gus said. "Anyway, she does it to all her boarders, not just me."

"But you all should do something!" Jessie exclaimed.

Gus shook his head. "The rent is cheap. Where else would I go that I could afford?" He tugged an envelope from his pocket. "That's not why I came. Andrew gave me

this the day before he disappeared. I think it's important. Maybe you kids can figure it out. I can't make heads or tails of it."

Henry took the envelope as Gus rose to leave.

"Won't you stay longer?" Violet asked, concerned about the man. "You could go to dinner with us."

"Thanks, but no," said Gus. He walked slowly down the block.

"Poor guy," said Jessie. "It must be awful to live there."

Henry was opening the envelope. He held up a piece of paper. On the paper were two sets of numbers.

Benny frowned. "What is that? Math?"

Violet stared at the paper. One column had single numbers in order — one, two, three, four, and so forth. The second column had rows of numbers all jumbled up.

"What does this mean?" she asked, perplexed.

"There's something about these numbers," Jessie said slowly. "But I can't think what."

"I know!" Henry cried. "The cat collars!" He pointed to the first row of numbers. "These are the numbers assigned to the cats."

"That makes sense," said Violet. "Nelda Pearson said the cats were numbered one, two, three, like that. But what is the second set of numbers?"

"The frequency of each cat's radio collar," Henry said. "When they want to tune in to a certain cat, the rangers use the numbers across from the cat's number."

Jessie tapped the bottom of the page. "Number Twenty-seven is circled in red. Something must be wrong with Cat Number Twenty-seven."

They all looked at one another.

"Andrew is on the trail of Cat Number Twenty-seven," said Violet.

"And tomorrow, we'll be on *his* trail," added Jessie.

CHAPTER 9

Big Lostmans Bay

The airboat roared like a low-flying plane, whizzing across the sawgrass.

It was such a strange boat, Violet thought, as the wind whipped her ponytails straight out behind her.

Mr. Osceola sat perched on a high seat, operating the controls just in front of the motor cage.

Before they had left that morning, Mr. Osceola helped the Aldens load their gear and explained what they should expect.

"The airboat is part plane, part boat," he

had told them. "It is designed to skim over the mud and sawgrass. I'll follow airboat routes cut through the sawgrass and down waterways."

On the dock, Henry had studied the map. From the Miccosukee Village, Irene's father planned to go through the Big Cypress National Preserve, heading southwest to a waterway called Big Lostmans Bay. The chickee where they'd set up camp was not too far from there.

Mr. Osceola had passed cuplike ear protectors out to everyone, then slipped a set over his own ears.

"What funny earmuffs," Benny had remarked.

"Sometimes I give three or four tours a day," Mr. Osceola had said. "These protect my hearing, so tap my shoulder if you want to ask me a question. Otherwise, I can't hear you. It will be loud, so you won't be able to hear each other very well once the motor starts."

Violet had sat beside Benny on the hard seat. The boat shot off all at once, frightening a flock of snowy egrets.

Benny laughed now with delight. He loved how fast they were going! Faster than any ride at the carnival!

"I wish I had worn my hair in braids," Jessie shouted to Irene, who sat next to her.

Irene shook her head. She couldn't hear. But the Miccosukee girl had wisely braided her thick black hair. Jessie's single ponytail was being blown all over.

Suddenly Mr. Osceola pointed to the right. Henry, sitting beside Grandfather in the back, saw a huge bull alligator slide into the water out of their way. He and Grandfather exchanged a look. This wasn't going to be an ordinary adventure.

Henry knew airboats disturbed wildlife. Mr. Osceola assured them he would drive carefully. Anyway, they weren't tourists on a joyride. They were on a mission to find Cat Number Twenty-seven, and, they hoped, Andrew Beldon.

After a while the roar suddenly quit. Mr. Osceola had switched off the engine. The blades of the propeller slowly whirled to a stop.

"Are we here?" asked Benny.

"No, I just thought you needed a break," said Mr. Osceola. "The noise and gas fumes can get to you. We're about halfway to Big Lostmans Bay."

"Big Lostmans Bay," repeated Violet. "Is that where you saw the man who looked like Andrew?"

Mr. Osceola nodded. "There are a lot of hammocks, creeks, and coves around there. It would be a good place to hide."

Or get lost in, Violet thought. She looked around. The Everglades surrounded them completely — miles of sharp-bladed saw-grass, dozens of humpy mangrove islands, an enchanted forest of orchids and other blooming flowers.

Someone tapped Violet's shoulder. It was Jessie.

"You ought to take pictures. We'll never see this again!"

"You're right." Violet held up her camera and began snapping photos.

The heat began to build. Jessie hadn't noticed how hot — or buggy — it was until they were sitting still. She swatted pesky insects in front of her face.

"Don't the bugs bother you?" she asked Irene.

"Yes, but I'm used to them," said Irene. "They are as much a part of the Glades as the herons and alligators."

"Everybody ready to take off?" Mr. Osceola called, slipping on his ear protectors.

"Yes!" said Jessie. The roar of the engine deafened her, but at least they were leaving the bugs behind.

Henry took out his compass. According to the magnetic needle, they were right on course. He admired Irene's father, who instinctively knew the maze of canals hacked into the sawgrass.

After a long while, sawgrass gave way to open water. Inlets and tiny hammocks dotted the river. After reaching a large hammock, Mr. Osceola once again turned off the engine.

"This is it," he announced, stepping

down from his high seat. "I'll help you set up base camp here."

"Where are we?" Benny asked. He felt a little dazed from the long, windy ride.

"On the map it's called Rogers River Bay Chickee," Mr. Osceola replied. "It's owned and maintained by the Park Service."

"I thought we were going to Big Lostmans Bay," said Henry.

"We are. We're here," said Irene. "This area of the Wilderness Waterway is part of Big Lostmans Bay." She helped her father anchor the boat.

"I have some canoes tied nearby," said Mr. Osceola. "So when I leave you, you'll still have transportation. You all know how to pole a canoe?"

"Irene gave us an excellent lesson the other day," Grandfather said. He and Henry began handing the supplies and packs to Irene and Mr. Osceola, who were on land.

Henry grunted from the weight of a red backpack. Benny's name tag dangled from the zipper. "Benny, what on earth is in your pack? It weighs a ton!"

"Things we might need," Benny replied secretively.

"Well, it feels like bricks!" Henry said.

When the airboat was unloaded, Mr. Osceola led the way through muck and weeds to the park chickee. Benny saw the wooden structure first.

"That's where we're going to sleep tonight!" he exclaimed. "Neat!" He loved the high wooden sides with built-in sleeping platforms.

"It is neat," Jessie agreed. "It's like that book we read. The one about the family stranded on the island and how they lived in a big tree house."

"This is like a boxcar tree house," Benny said, scrambling up the side.

Mr. Osceola handed up some of their gear. "Remember," he cautioned, "you are in the backcountry. Always wear mosquito repellent. Keep your arms and legs covered. Don't forget a hat or your snakebite kits. At night, we'll drape our sleeping bags or hammocks in mosquito netting."

"I brought plenty," Grandfather told Mr.

Osceola. "And Jessie packed enough insect spray for ten families."

"And lunch," she said, unloading a large pack. "Mrs. Johnson fixed us sandwiches this morning. Nothing that would spoil in the heat."

Sitting cross-legged on the chickee, everyone ate peanut butter sandwiches, potato chips, and ripe mangoes. Irene contributed pumpkin bread to the meal. A thermos of still-cold iced tea tasted wonderful.

For dinner that night, Jessie and Grandfather had brought prepackaged meals that didn't require heating. They would drink bottled water.

When they had safely put the food in animal-proof containers, Benny asked, "Are we going to explore now?"

"Yes," said Irene. "This isn't where Daddy saw the man who looked like Ranger Beldon. We'll only sleep here tonight."

They all clambered back into the airboat and were soon flying over open water. As they approached a small hammock, Mr. Osceola turned off the engine.

"I keep a couple of canoes hidden here," he said, wading through the water. He pulled back some branches to reveal a pair of canoes. "You can't go everywhere in an airboat."

He pulled the canoes forward, so the Aldens could reach them.

Irene, Grandfather, and Benny took one canoe. Henry, Jessie, and Violet claimed the other.

"I will leave you now," said Mr. Osceola, once again at the controls of his airboat. "I must get back to the village for my tour."

"When will you come back?" asked Grandfather.

"Probably late today," said Mr. Osceola. "You're in good hands. Irene knows as much as I do about the Glades. Good luck. I hope you find Andrew Beldon."

So do we, thought Jessie, watching Mr. Osceola push his airboat back so he could take off without splashing their canoes.

When the airboat roar died and all they heard were birds calling, Irene said, "Well, let's go. Daddy saw the man on the next hammock. We have a lot of daylight to look for whoever it was."

They poled silently through the wilderness. Henry listened to the plop of a turtle sliding into the water, the flip-flop of fish jumping, the buzz of bugs. Even Benny was quiet, enjoying the closeness of nature.

Henry thought about the elusive Florida panther. From the pictures he'd seen of the beautiful cat, Henry understood why the ranger wanted to protect the last remaining animals. But Andrew's love of the big cats could have brought him big trouble.

Irene poled the lead boat into a tight cove. Getting out, she tugged the front end of the boat up onto a mangrove root. Henry and Jessie slipped over the side and waded through shallow water to secure their canoe next to Irene's.

"Yuck," said Jessie. "I'm all wet!"

"But at least you're cool," Violet said. "Look on the bright side!" She had never seen such wild beauty. She quickly finished a roll of film and reloaded her camera.

But as they walked farther, the scenery

became dark and eerie. The foliage was so thick, sunlight was blocked out. Violet couldn't take any more pictures.

"It's creepy in here," Benny whispered.

Jessie couldn't agree more. Instead of drying out in the heat, her jeans stayed wet because it was so humid. Lagging behind the others, she tried to find a ray of stray sunlight to walk in.

Then she heard it. A slithering sound.

She hurried to the front of the line, where Grandfather and Irene were walking.

"I heard something!" she whispered.

"What?" asked Grandfather.

"I don't know," Jessie said. It didn't sound like a snake. But then things sounded different in the Glades.

Irene made a small motion with her hands. "It was probably a turtle."

"It's not a turtle," Jessie insisted. She listened carefully. "I can still hear it!"

Everyone stopped. The soft slithering noise stopped, too, at least a beat behind them.

Forgetting her fear of snakes, Jessie ran back to the clearing.

"Here's a footprint!" she cried. "It's not an animal print! It belongs to a person!"

"It could be one of ours," Irene said. "We're all wearing shoes."

Benny knelt close to the track. "Not like this one." From his red pack, which he had brought along, he lifted out an object. It was the plaster cast of the footprint.

"I told you this would come in handy." He set the cast next to the muddy print.

The prints were identical.

Everyone could see the distinctive V mark on the sole.

Just then Violet whirled. She saw a man half hidden behind a mangrove root. "There he is!" she cried.

With Henry in the lead this time, the children ran after the man. They quickly grabbed him. The man did not fight back.

"Good job," said Grandfather when he caught up to them.

"It's the bushy-haired man!" Violet exclaimed. "The one who's been following us!"

"And me, too," said a strange voice.

CHAPTER 10

Benny's Second Wish

A second man stepped into the clearing, his slim figure striped by shadows. He clasped a plastic box with a short antenna in both hands. He was younger than the other man and his hair was blond and straight.

Benny stared at the two men. The bushy-haired man also had a plastic box. The men glared at each other.

"I bet you're Andrew Beldon," Benny said to the younger man.

The blond man grinned. "You're right! And who might you be?"

"I'm Benny Alden," he replied. "We came to find you."

As Grandfather came forward, Andrew's face lit up. "Mr. Alden!" he cried. "What are you doing here in the Everglades?"

"Just what my grandson said," Grandfather answered. "Your father called me. He said he hadn't heard from you and he was worried. So he asked me to come down and look around. These are my grandchildren. You've already met Benny. This is Henry, Violet, and Jessie."

"We thought something had happened to you," Jessie said. "Melanie Harper wouldn't tell us anything."

Andrew wrinkled his nose. "That's a long story. Didn't think I'd notice you, did you?" he said to the bushy-haired man.

The other man tried to slip away, but tripped over a mangrove root. He fell, dropping his plastic box in the muck. Andrew crossed the clearing and picked up the box.

"It's almost like yours," Benny commented. "How come you both are out here with those boxes?"

Henry knew. "Those are electronic receivers. Andrew and this other guy were tracking a panther."

"Cat Number Twenty-seven," Violet finished.

Andrew stared at her in astonishment. "That's right, but how did you know?"

"Gus Hummer gave us the paper with the numbers on it," Violet said. "The one that listed the cats and their signals. You had circled Number Twenty-seven in red."

"Good old Gus. I told him, if I didn't come back in a week, to take the paper to the park authorities," Andrew said. "But why would he take it to you kids instead?"

"Melanie kept giving us the runaround," Jessie said. "So we found out where you lived and met Gus."

"Obviously Gus trusted you kids. But how did you know about the signal collars?" Andrew was clearly impressed.

Jessie replied, "We talked to your partner, Nelda Pearson. She told us how you felt about the panthers."

"Your grandchildren are very smart," Andrew said to Grandfather.

"Yes, they've solved quite a few mysteries," Grandfather said. "But I wish you had called your father, Andy. He's been very worried."

"I know and I'm sorry. I was away longer than I intended." The ranger kept one foot on the bushy-haired man's leg so he couldn't get up and run away.

"Because of this man?" Benny asked.

"Yes, we were both tracking the signals of Cat Number Twenty-seven," said Andrew. "Twenty-seven — I call him Runner because he's fast — is a healthy male cat. I started to worry about him a few weeks ago, when I noticed his movements were becoming erratic."

"Err-what?" Benny asked.

Andrew explained. "The cats wander within their own territories. Those territories can cover up to two hundred square miles. Runner kept invading other panthers' areas. He acted like he was lost. Or like something was after him. I figured he was in some sort of trouble. So I decided to track him and make sure he was okay."

"Why didn't you tell anyone?" asked Henry.

"I didn't have time," said Andrew. "And I had a suspicion I wanted to keep to myself until I had proof."

"What were you suspicious of?" Violet wanted to know.

"I believed Runner was being hunted — and not by another animal." Andrew frowned at the bushy-haired man. "Soon I was tracking both the cat and a man. It wasn't hard, since this guy has a similar receiving device. Plus he left footprints all over the place."

"Like this one!" Benny proudly showed Andrew the plaster cast of the boot mark.

"Boy, you kids are real pros!" Andrew said admiringly.

"We've been seeing this guy everywhere," Jessie told Andrew. "He followed us up on the observation tower at Shark Valley. And we've seen him in the snack shop at the Miccosukee Village."

Irene scowled at the man on the ground. "I've seen you hanging around, too. Who are you?"

Sighing, the man sat up. "My name is Ned Fry. I work for a rich man who owns a private zoo. He wanted a Florida panther in his zoo. So he hired me to catch one."

"That's terrible!" Violet exclaimed. "There are so few cats left in the wild. And you were going to steal one!"

"It's called poaching," Andrew said. "Ned Fry isn't the first to poach in the Everglades. Some people will pay lots of money to have an alligator, a crocodile, even a Florida panther in their personal collections."

"I'm also a radio operator. It wasn't hard to find the radio frequencies on the cats' collars," Ned said. "Soon I began tracking Cat Number Twenty-seven."

"But we kept seeing you at the visitors' center," said Benny. "You were hiding behind the postcard rack!"

Ned went on, realizing the jig was up. "I'm not that familiar with the Glades and had to keep going back into town for supplies and to the visitors' centers for maps. One day I heard you kids talking about Andrew Beldon."

"You looked like a tourist," Violet said accusingly.

"I knew Andrew was in the Glades," said Ned. His brow was sweating. "I had to keep using disguises so the park people and you Aldens wouldn't recognize me. Once I figured you kids were looking for Andrew, I had to watch out for him and keep my eye on you, too!"

"Busy man," Irene commented. She tilted her head toward a sound.

"I don't think Ned will be so busy in the future," said Andrew. "That's your father's airboat, isn't it, Irene?"

"Yes, he said he'd stay on the chickee with us tonight. We're camping out." She put her hands on her hips and looked at Andrew. "That *was* you Daddy saw, wasn't it? Why didn't you answer him?"

"I couldn't," Andrew explained. "I still hadn't found Ned or Runner. I didn't want to get Mr. Osceola involved in case I had trouble with Ned."

The airboat roared into the clearing, then was quiet. Mr. Osceola waded through the shallow water to the mangrove hammock.

"Well," he said. "I see our party is a little larger. Good to see you, Andrew. You could have called back to me."

Andrew shook his head regretfully. "Sorry, but I couldn't risk Runner's life. I'm afraid I've caused people to worry and my boss to be upset with me, but the cats come first."

Mr. Osceola nudged Ned Fry's shoe. "I've seen you sneaking around. You were after that cat, weren't you? You left a trail a mile wide — footprints, snapped branches."

"What will happen now?" asked Jessie. It was getting late and the bugs were getting to be even more of a nuisance.

Andrew helped Ned Fry to his feet. "Ned will have to take a little trip back to the ranger station, where he will be charged for attempted poaching. That's a very serious crime in this state. The Florida panther is the state animal."

"What about our camp-out?" Benny didn't want to skip the fun part. Not before he had a chance to have his second wish granted.

Grandfather had a plan. "Suppose the kids and I set up the camp. Andy and Mr. Osceola can escort Mr. Fry to the ranger station. Andy, it would be great if you could come back. *After* you call your father."

"I promise! I'll come back in my own air-boat and give Mr. Osceola a break."

"And I'll return for you all in the morning," said Mr. Osceola. "It would be easier to return in two airboats."

Andrew grasped one of Ned Fry's arms above the elbow. Irene's father did the same with Ned's other arm. They led him out to the airboat. The engine roared to life and soon the men were gone.

"Well," said Grandfather. "The mystery is solved. I suppose we should canoe over to our chickee and set up camp."

Henry and Irene pushed their canoes into the water and everyone climbed aboard.

"Not all the mysteries," said Jessie as she

poled. "What about Melanie Harper? And Andrew's landlady? There are still lots of questions."

"Maybe we'll get the answers when Andrew comes back," said Henry. He was thinking of Andrew's bravery, coming into the Everglades alone to protect a wildcat. Andrew had entered the private world of an animal people rarely saw.

It didn't take the Aldens long to fix camp. Irene and Benny each strung hammocks across the poles. The others preferred sleeping bags, which they'd unroll when it was bedtime.

They were preparing supper when Andrew came roaring back in a different airboat. He crossed the island quickly and climbed up into the chickee.

"Was your boss mad?" Violet asked him.

"Yes," Andrew said. "But when I brought in the poacher and told him about Runner, he decided not to fire me. I have my old job back."

Jessie looked surprised. "Melanie was so sure she was going to get your job."

Andrew opened a container of trail mix. "Melanie was sure of a lot of things. We used to date. At first I thought she was nice, but then I realized she only wanted to get a better job. So I stopped seeing her. It made her really mad."

"Mad enough to lie about hearing from you," Jessie said, popping a piece of peeled orange into her mouth.

Andrew nodded. "Melanie was always jealous of Nelda. Nelda is a real friend — she cares as much about the cats as I do."

"How come you didn't tell Nelda about your feeling about Runner?" asked Henry.

"I didn't have any real proof," said Andrew. "In fact, I didn't have any proof until today, when Ned confessed in front of all of us. He told the same story at the ranger station."

Jessie mentioned Old Lady Applegate, Andrew's landlady. "We think she was stealing from your room."

Andrew shrugged. "She probably was. Small change, little things she could sell at the flea market. I know she's taken from Gus and the other people."

"That's terrible," said Violet. "Stealing from people. Gus said he can't afford to live anywhere else."

"He can't." Andrew sighed. "I keep forgetting that people need looking after, too, not just panthers. When I go home, I'll make sure things change at the boarding-house."

Night fell softly around them. After they ate, Andrew told them stories about the Everglades. Irene added tales from Micco-sukee culture.

Henry asked Irene if he could write to her. Irene replied she'd be glad to be Henry's pen pal.

Then it was time to go to bed. Henry, Grandfather, Jessie, Violet, and Andrew un-rolled their sleeping bags. The girls slept on the sleeping platforms. Irene showed Benny how to scramble into his hammock. He nearly fell twice, but at last he was rocking gently. Everyone was swathed in mosquito netting.

It was anything but quiet. All kinds of in-sects made noises from the trees. Night-birds called. A bull alligator bellowed in the distance.

Then, suddenly, came a scream. It wasn't a human scream nor was it a cry of distress.

Benny sat up, nearly spinning in his hammock. "What was *that*?" he cried.

"That," answered Andrew Beldon from the darkness, "was a Florida panther."

"Was it Runner?" Benny asked.

"It could be," said Andrew.

Grandfather said, "People go for years without ever seeing or hearing a panther. This is a special moment."

Benny settled back in his hammock. Grandfather was right. He'd gotten his second, even better wish.

He'd heard a panther. He didn't think he'd ever *see* one, but at least he knew one was nearby.

The Aldens had solved another mystery. Tomorrow, if they were lucky, they'd be off on another great adventure!

GERTRUDE CHANDLER WARNER discovered when she was teaching that many readers who like an exciting story could find no books that were both easy and fun to read. She decided to try to meet this need, and her first book, *The Boxcar Children*, quickly proved she had succeeded.

Miss Warner drew on her own experiences to write the mystery. As a child she spent hours watching trains go by on the tracks opposite her family home. She often dreamed about what it would be like to set up housekeeping in a caboose or freight car — the situation the Alden children find themselves in.

When Miss Warner received requests for more adventures involving Henry, Jessie, Violet, and Benny Alden, she began additional stories. In each, she chose a special setting and introduced unusual or eccentric characters who liked the unpredictable.

While the mystery element is central to each of Miss Warner's books, she never thought of them as strictly juvenile mysteries. She liked to stress the Aldens' independence and resourcefulness and their solid New England devotion to using up and making do. The Aldens go about most of their adventures with as little adult supervision as possible — something else that delights young readers.

Miss Warner lived in Putnam, Connecticut, until her death in 1979. During her lifetime, she received hundreds of letters from girls and boys telling her how much they liked her books.